The Toy Town Parade

HarperCollins *Children's Books*

It was a very exciting day in Toyland. A very special event that only happens once a year was about to take place!

"Noddy! Noddy!" called Master Tubby Bear. "Have you forgotten what day it is?"

"Of course not!" answered Noddy. "Today is the Toy Town Parade!"

"Then why aren't you down at the Town Hall?" asked Master Tubby Bear.

"I will be – I have to pick up Big-Ears first. He wants to watch the parade," replied Noddy.

"You better hurry, Noddy! The parade is starting soon and I'm going to be in it! Right at the front, I'll bet!" cried Master Tubby Bear as he skipped off.

A few minutes later, Noddy was driving Big-Ears to Toy Town.

"I love Parade Day, Big-Ears. I do, I do, I do!" Noddy said, excitedly.

"You funny little Noddy!" chuckled Big-Ears.

Noddy was so excited that he sang a song:
Red balloons
Cake and lemonade
Let's get ready
For the big parade!
Toys will march
Trumpets will be played
All of us will
Join in the parade!

By the time Noddy and Big-Ears arrived at the Town Hall, crowds were already gathering. Everyone was chattering and giggling in excitement as Mr Plod tried to get them in order.

"Folks, please quiet down. That's enough, now. Listen up, everyone. OK, let's have some quiet!" Mr Plod addressed the crowd.

"Hello, Mr Plod!" called Noddy. "What's going on? Is it time for the parade to start yet?"

"Yes, it is," answered Mr Plod, frustrated, "but nobody will listen!"

Mr Plod turned back to the crowd.

"Quiet!"

Everyone stopped talking.

"That's better. Now, before we can begin, we must decide who will be first and lead the parade," Mr Plod informed them.

Everybody shouted at once because they all
wanted to lead the parade.

"Me, pick me!" shouted Martha Monkey.

"I want to go first!" cried Mr Wobbly Man.

"No, it's my turn!" argued Master Tubby Bear.

"Me first, me!" Skippy Skittle said.

"I should go first!" said Martha Monkey.

"But you were first last year!" Mr Sparks reminded her.

"Right!" she replied, jumping up and down, "so I should be first every year!"

Big-Ears noticed that Noddy had not been shouting with all the others.

"What's wrong, Noddy?" Big-Ears asked him. "Don't you want to be first too?"

"No, I don't care if I'm number three or seven or fourteen or twenty-six! I just want to be in the parade," smiled Noddy.

"Ah, that is very sensible of you, Noddy," Big-Ears told him.

"I never get to be first," Tessie Bear said, glumly.

"I was last, last year!" Master Tubby Bear told everyone.

"Maybe we should vote on it!" suggested Mr Jumbo.

"Then I vote you go last!" jeered Martha Monkey.

Mr Plod tried to stop the crowd getting out of hand. "There will be no parade if you don't work together. Not everyone can be first!"

"Look at all the time we have wasted, arguing!" Noddy pointed out. "Since we can't decide, let's ask Big-Ears to choose who will go first."

"Excellent idea, Noddy!" agreed Mr Jumbo, and Big-Ears chuckled. "Well, everybody, shall we let Big-Ears decide?"

Everybody agreed with Noddy.

"Very well," said Mr Plod. "Since Big-Ears always
knows the right thing to do, he shall pick who
will go first in our parade."

"Thank you, thank you," started Big-Ears.
"Now, will everyone please stand still so I can
look and decide."

Big-Ears thought hard and scratched his head
as he looked at the crowd.

"Woof woof!" barked Bumpy Dog.

"Shhh, Bumpy Dog!" Noddy told him.
"You be a good dog and sit right here."

"I have chosen," Big-Ears stated.

"Who? Who is first?" everybody asked as
they crowded round. "Tell us, Big-Ears!"

"Because he was the only one who was not loud or pushy – and because he didn't care if he was first or last – I pick Noddy to lead the parade!" Big-Ears told everyone.

The crowd gasped and chuckled, and then everyone cheered and applauded.

"Thank you, Big-Ears!" Noddy cried, excitedly. "And thank you, all my friends, for letting me be first!"

"Now, listen carefully," instructed Mr Plod. "Big-Ears will explain how the parade will run."

"Everyone who wants to watch the parade will stand here, on the steps of the Town Hall. Everyone who wants to be in the parade will line up by the Ice Cream Parlour where I will give you a number," Big-Ears explained. "You will then march around the Town Square, stop here in front of the steps – where you will do something clever – then return to the Ice Cream Parlour."

"…where we will celebrate with banana splits and ice cream sundaes!" added Miss Pink Cat.

"Thank you, Miss Pink Cat," nodded Big-Ears. "You will be number two in the parade,"

"Oh! Two is my favourite number!" cried Miss Pink Cat.

"Tessie Bear, you are number three," Big-Ears informed her.

"I love number three! Three is my lucky number!" Tessie Bear cheered.

"What's my number, Big-Ears?" asked Master Tubby Bear.

"You shall follow Tessie as number four, Master Tubby Bear," replied Big-Ears.

"Why can't I be number four?" moaned Martha Monkey.

"Because, Martha Monkey, I have saved number five for you!" Big-Ears told her, with a smile.

"All right," finished Big-Ears, "as I call the rest of the numbers, please go over to the Ice Cream Parlour and line up. The Toy Town Parade is about to begin!"

"Make way for Noddy!" shouted Noddy, as he drove through in his little taxi. "Parp-parp!"

"Ooh!" sighed Miss Pink Cat, "I love the parade!"

"It's like I always say," Tessie Bear gasped, "it is a perfectly perfect day for the Toy Town Parade!"

"Mr Plod, you are number nine," Big-Ears
continued.

"Nine! After eight and before ten! Very
smart!" said Mr Plod, happily.

"Wonderful!" said Mr Wobbly Man, as Big-Ears
told him he would be number ten in the parade.

Over by the Town Hall steps, it was Martha Monkey's turn to do a trick.

"Joke time!" called Martha. "Want to see a pair of yellow slippers?" she asked, as she brought out two bananas.

"Get it? Banana peels … slippers!" she laughed.

"Whee!" laughed the Skittle children as they ran into Mr Wobbly Man and tumbled over.

"Whoa! Whoa! I hate it when that happens!" said Mr Wobbly Man, with a grin on his face. "Except on Parade Day!"

Big-Ears turned to Mr Jumbo and Clockwork Mouse, who were the last two to join the parade.

"You two get to do the big finish for the parade," Big-Ears told them.

"Thank you, Big-Ears. We'll try to make it a good one, then!" Mr Jumbo smiled.

"I think I'll run over to the Town Hall and watch the end of the parade. Good luck!" said Big-Ears as he ran off.

Outside the Town Hall, Clockwork Mouse had
climbed onto Mr Jumbo's head for their big finale:
a balancing act. It was going very well until Mr
Jumbo got a tickle in his trunk.

"AAH – AAH – AAH – CHOO!" sneezed
Mr Jumbo.

"Ahhhhh!" squealed Clockwork Mouse as he
tumbled off Mr Jumbo's head.

Luckily, Mr Jumbo caught him in his trunk. But
nobody cheered.

Big-Ears arrived at the Town Hall just after Clockwork Mouse's tumble.

"Hmm…" wondered Big-Ears, "what have we here? Can it be..?"

"Woof woof!" barked Bumpy Dog as he trotted up to Big-Ears.

"Bumpy Dog!" chuckled Big-Ears. "Are you the only one here?"

"Everyone was so excited to be in the parade," laughed Big-Ears, "that nobody was here to watch the parade! Except for you, Bumpy Dog. So, how did you like it?"

"Woof woof woof!" replied Bumpy Dog.

"Maybe next year, you can be in the parade too, and we'll all watch you!" Big-Ears grinned as Bumpy Dog jumped up and licked his face.

First published in Great Britain by HarperCollins Children's Books in 2006
HarperCollins Children's Books is a division of HarperCollins Publishers Ltd,
77-85 Fulham Palace Road, Hammersmith, London W6 8JB

3 5 7 9 10 8 6 4 2

ISBN-10: 0-00-722339-0
ISBN-13: 978-0-00-722339-8

A CIP catalogue for this title is available from the British Library.

Printed and bound by
Printing Express Ltd, Hong Kong

make way for
NODDY
™

Collect them all!

Noddy and the Treasure Map
ISBN 0-00-721056-6

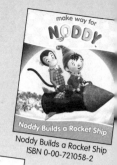

Noddy Builds a Rocket Ship
ISBN 0-00-721058-2

Noddy's Pet Chicken
ISBN 0-00-721057-4

Goblins Above
ISBN 0-00-721059-0

Hold on to Your Hat, Noddy
ISBN 0 00 712243 8

A Grey Day in Toy Town
ISBN 0 00 722336 6

The Magic Powder
ISBN 0 00 715101 2

Skittle in the Middle
ISBN 0 00 722337 4

Bounce Alert in Toy Town
ISBN 0 00 715103 9

The Goblins' Stopwatch
ISBN 0 00 722338 2

**And send off for your free Noddy poster (rrp £3.99).
Simply collect 4 tokens and complete the coupon below.**

✂

TOKEN

Name: _____

Address: _____

_____

_____

e-mail: _____

❏ Tick here if you do not wish to receive further information about children's books.

Send coupon to: **Noddy Poster Offer, PO Box 142, Horsham, RH13 5FJ.**

Terms and conditions: proof of sending cannot be considered proof of receipt. Not redeemable for cash. 28 days delivery. Offer open to UK residents only.

Make Way For Noddy videos now available at all good retailers.

UNIVERSAL